For Jack, Ellie, Lloyd and Lewis – J.P

THERE'S ALWAYS ONE!
by John Prater
British Library Cataloguing in Publication Data
A catalogue record of this book is available from the British Library.
ISBN 0 340 85533 9 (HB)
ISBN 0 340 85534 7 (PB)

First edition published 2004
10 9 8 7 6 5 4 3 2

Published by Hodder Children's Books, a division of Hodder Headline Limited,
338 Euston Road, London NW1 3BH

There's Always One!

John Prater

Hodder
Children's
Books

A division of Hodder Headline Limited

It was a hot summer's day – perfect for a trip to the beach.
Dad counted the bunnies.

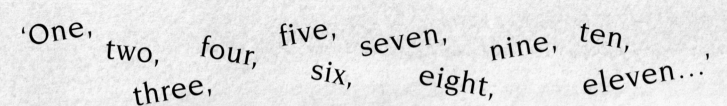

'One, two, three, four, five, six, seven, eight, nine, ten, eleven...'

Jacob was missing!

'There's always one,' said Mum.

'Jacob!'

Jacob came clattering down the stairs.
'Sorry,' he gasped. 'Just packing!'
Mum laughed. 'Do you really need
all of that?'

'All of what?' said Jacob.

When they arrived at the beach, everyone was very excited. They settled in a sheltered spot and started to change.

But not Jacob!

'There's always one!' sighed Dad.

He gave Jacob a big rubber ring. '**Now** you can swim,' he said.

But one wasn't enough for Jacob!

And two was too many!

'There's always one,' laughed Dad again.

'Come on, you two,'
shouted Mum.
'Let's dig!'

Jacob built a sandcastle.
It was big and tall and it had a moat.

Sadly,   it didn't last

'There's
always
one!'
sighed Mum.
'Come and have
some lunch.'

very long...

But Jacob wasn't hungry.

Dad was cross.

'There's always one,' he said.
'Eat up quietly.
Then it's rest time!'

But Jacob wasn't tired.
'Sleeping is boring,'
he sighed.
'I want to go
exploring!'

So, when the others were all fast asleep,
off he went.
I won't go far, he thought.

Some time later, the others awoke.
Something was different...
Someone had taken away the beach.
There was water everywhere.

They were stuck!

HELP!

Mum started to count:

'One, two, three, four, five, six, seven, eight, nine, ten, eleven...

Oh no!' she shouted.

'Behind you,'
cried a little voice.

Jacob had found a cave.
'Look there's daylight,'
he called. 'Follow me!'

'Phew,' said Dad. 'That was close.'
'It was,' laughed Mum, 'we nearly
had to swim back.'

'But there's always one, isn't there!

Well done, Jacob!'